Oxford University Press, Walton Street, Oxford OX2 6DP
OXFORD LONDON GLASGOW
NEW YORK TORONTO MELBOURNE WELLINGTON
KUALA LUMPUR SINGAPORE HONG KONG TOKYO
DELHI BOMBAY CALCUTTA MADRAS KARACHI
NAIROBI DAR ES SALAAM CAPE TOWN

© *Brian Wildsmith 1978*   ISBN 0 19 279724 7

First published 1978   Reprinted 1980

Printed in Hong Kong by Hip Shing Offset Printing Factory

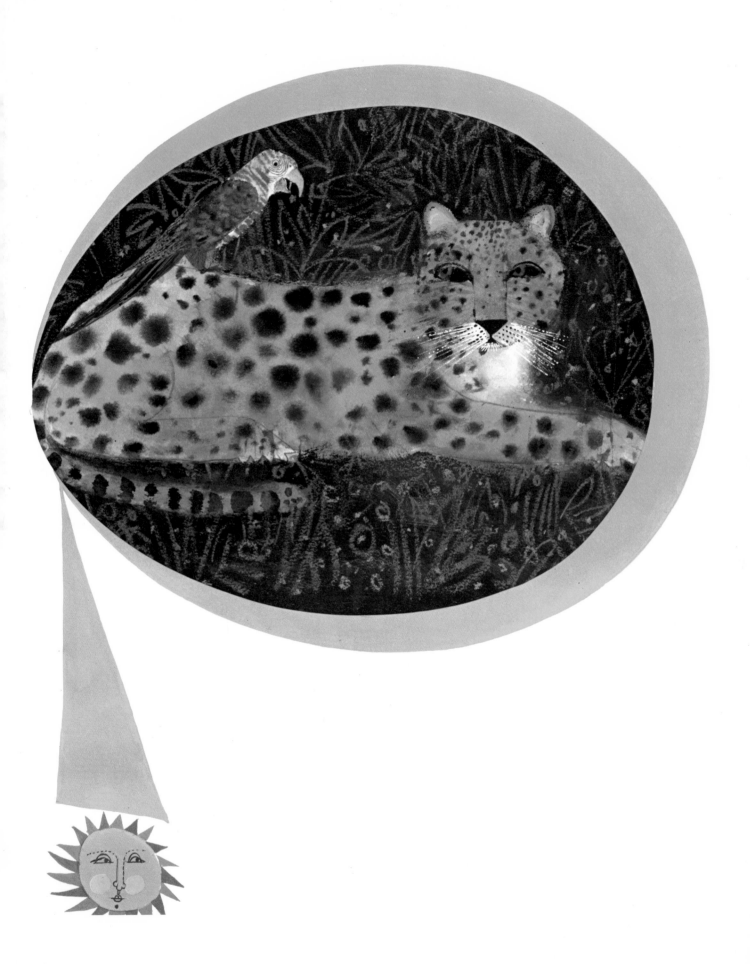

Oxford University Press

OXFORD NEW YORK TORONTO MELBOURNE

Brian Wildsmith

What the Moon saw

The Moon was complaining to the Sun that she had never really seen the world that lay below.

'I,' said the Sun, 'have seen everything, and I will show you some of the many things to be found there.'

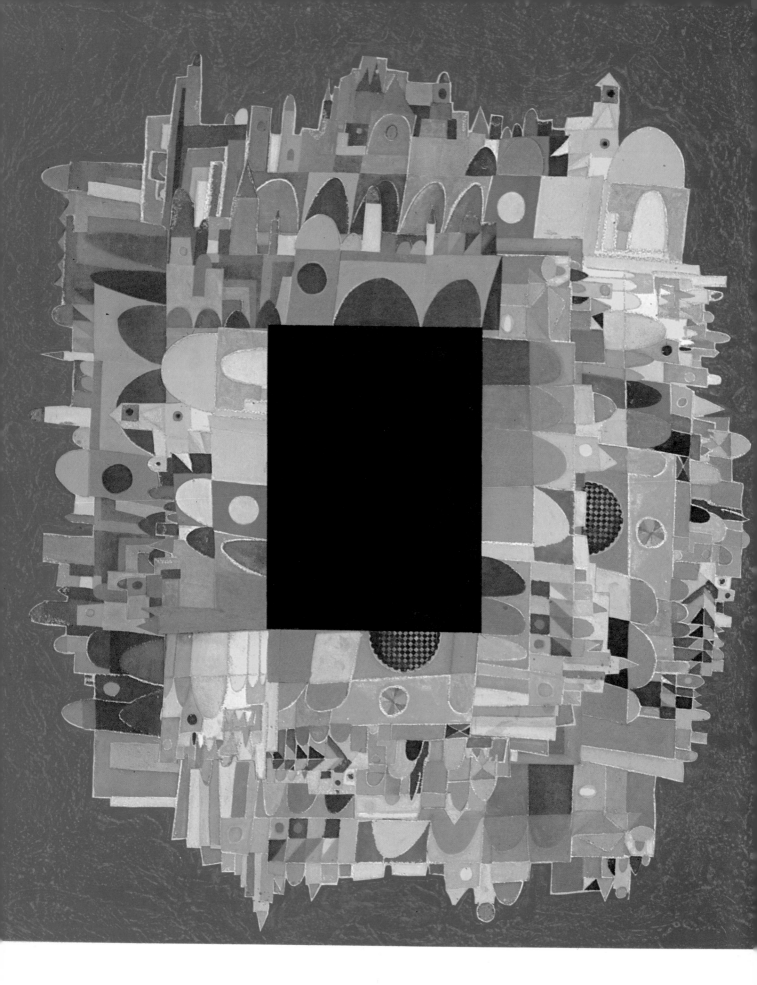

'That is a city. It has **many** houses and buildings.'

'There is a village. It has **few** houses.'

'This is the **outside** of a house,

and if you peep through the windows
you can see the **inside**.'

'Look further and you will see a **big** forest,

and in it is a **little** flower.'

'Here we look at a dog from the **front**,

and here from the **back**.'

'This elephant is a **heavy** beast,

but this bird is very **light**.'

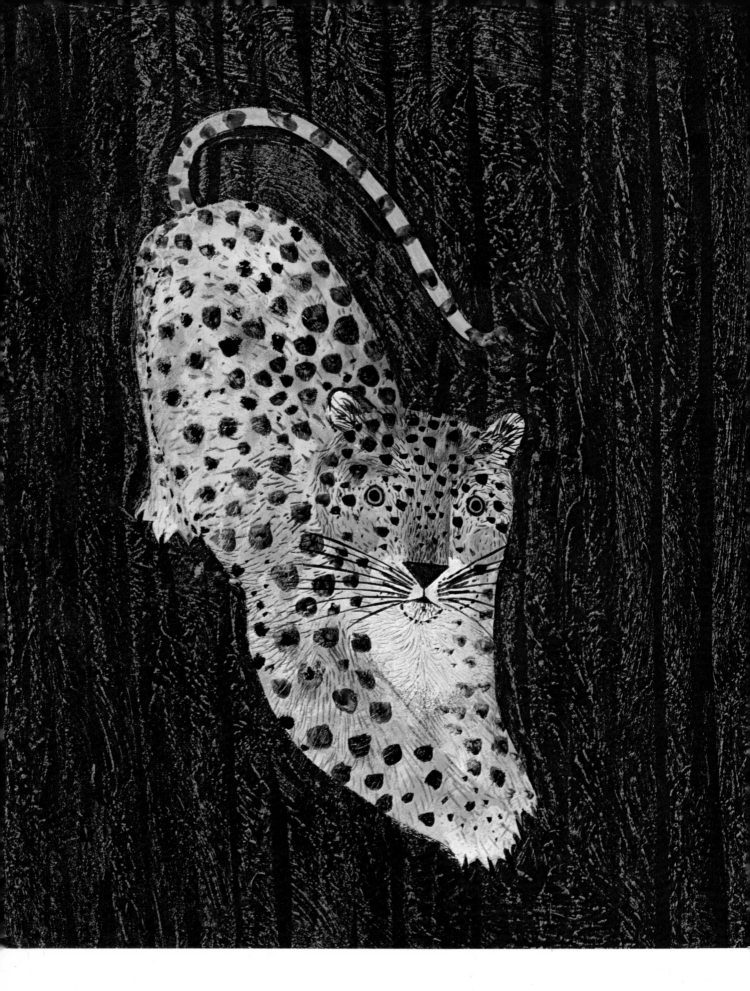

'The leopard's coat is **patterned** with spots,

the mane of the lion is **plain**.'

'Here is a **fat** hippopotamus,

and there is a **thin** lizard.'

'A **feathered** pelican,

and a **furry** llama.'

'The giraffe's neck is **long**,

but the racoon has a **short** neck.'

'Look at the **fierce** tiger,

and the **timid** rabbit.'

'A **weak** kitten,

a **strong** bear.'

'When running the cheetah is **fast**,

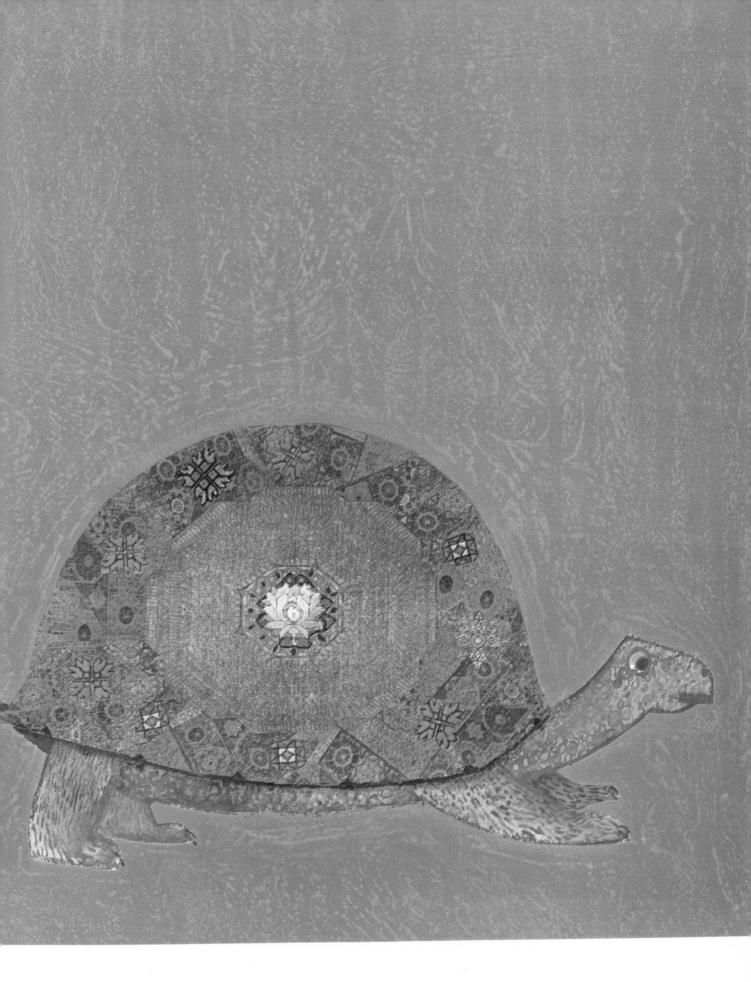

but the tortoise is always **slow**.'

'Isn't that all wonderful to see,' said the Sun,